Lucy
in the
City

**A Story About
Developing Spatial
Thinking Skills**

by **Julie Dillemuth, PhD**

illustrated by
Laura Wood

Magination Press • **Washington, DC** • **American Psychological Association**

Lucy woke up from a good day's sleep. She followed her Papa, her Mama, her sister, and her brother out of their cozy den.

They ran up streets.

They slinked down alleys.

They tiptoed through backyards.

They headed for the best garbage bins in town.
But all Lucy noticed was the *bob, bob, bob*
of her brother's tail in front of her nose.

Lucy rummaged in the rubbish.
PEANUT BUTTER!

She scurried behind a
garbage bin, before the others
could see her treasure.

And when Papa called out,
"Time to go!" Lucy didn't notice.

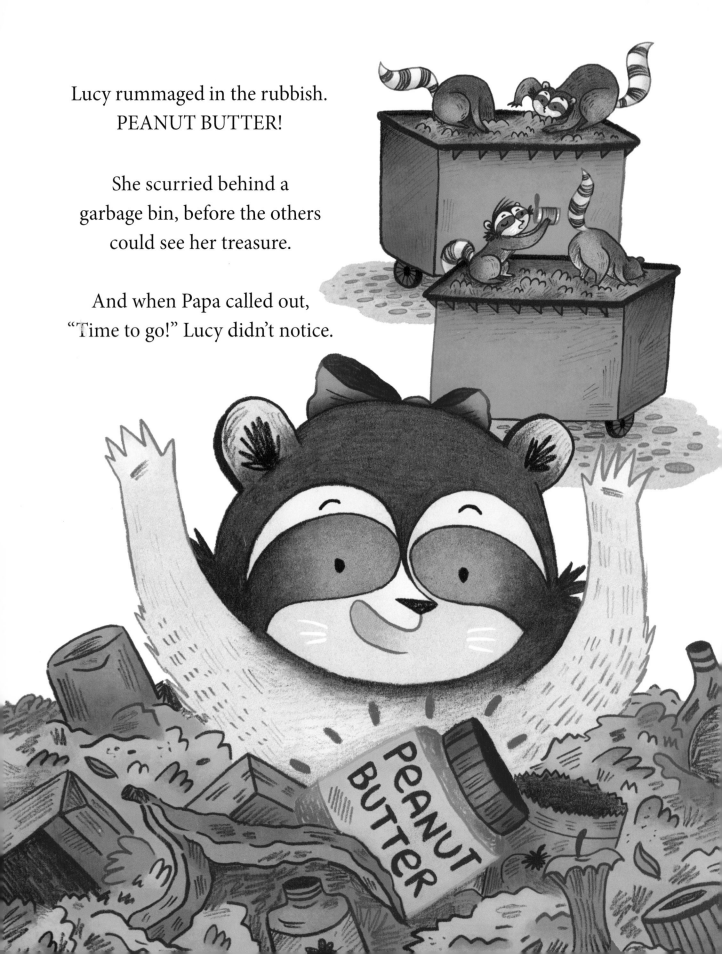

When she had licked the jar clean, Lucy looked around.
"Where is everyone?" she asked.

"Who, who?"
an owl called out.

"My family," Lucy said.
"Did they leave without me?"

Lucy looked up at the dark night sky.
She had never noticed how it glittered full of stars.
Her eyes welled full of tears. Her whiskers drooped.
"How will I get home?" she sniffed.

She sniffed again. Popcorn. Lucy knew that scent.
She had smelled it along the way.

If she could find it again, she would be one step closer to home.

Lucy looked around, but she wasn't sure where to go. Her whiskers twitched.

"Owl, can you fly up high, and see where there is popcorn nearby?" she called.

"Movie theater up ahead!"
the owl said. "It's one block east
and three blocks north."

Lucy ran one block east and three blocks north to the movie theater.

She had never noticed how the popcorn crunched under her feet,
and how the candy stuck to her paws. Yum, but yuck.

Lucy licked her paw, trying to remember other things she had passed.
Finding those things again would take her back home, step by step.

She looked around for something to drink. "That's it!" she cried.

"Owl, can you fly up high, and see
where there is water nearby?"
"A pond in the park, right this way!"
the owl called down. "Two blocks
east and two blocks south."

Lucy ran two blocks east and two blocks south, to the park. She had never noticed how the moonlight shimmered on the quiet pond. She swished her tail.

Where had she been before
the pond in the park?

Her mouth watered.

"Owl, can you fly up high,
and see where there are
cookies nearby?" Lucy asked.

"A bakery, over here! Three blocks east,
and one block south," called the owl.

Lucy ran the three blocks east and one block south to the bakery. She had never noticed the bakers busy inside, late into the night. Her feet flew over the pavement as she ran past the bakery.

She did not stop. She heard the sound of rushing water and knew where to go.

There was a bridge across the river
two more blocks south. "We did it!
Thank you, Owl!" she called.

Lucy ran two blocks south to the bridge. She was almost home.

She ran up a street…

Slinked down an alley…

And tiptoed through a backyard.

Lucy found her cozy den,
and her Papa, her Mama,
her sister, and her brother,
just as the sun came up.

Note to Parents, Caregivers, and Professionals

Think about a recent trip you made—perhaps to a school, your workplace, or a store. How did you get there and back? You probably have some sort of mental picture of the route you took and what you saw along the way. When we navigate, we search our "mental map" of an area to figure out where to go. Young children are just starting to develop this ability, as well as other important spatial thinking skills. Spatial thinking is how we think about and understand the world around us, and use concepts of space for problem solving. Thinking analytically about spatial relationships is something we do every day—by navigating somewhere, putting dishes away in a kitchen cabinet, or playing sports, for example. We often take these skills for granted because we use them automatically. This type of thinking is also central to many professions, particularly science and technology fields.

Types of spatial thinking include:
- **Spatial relationships:** understanding how different objects relate to each other in space—for example, picturing how something with moving parts works, constructing something, setting the table, or packing a bag.
- **Spatial memory:** remembering where things are.
- **Spatial representations:** reading maps, diagrams, and charts.
- **Spatial language:** understanding and using terms such as o*n, above, below, near, next to,* and *between.*
- **Sense of direction:** navigating or finding your way.

Early exposure to spatial concepts can help foster this type of cognitive development in children, as well as boost their math and science learning as they progress through school. Practice can help improve these skills at any age.

How This Book Can Help

Lucy in the City tells the story of a raccoon who, distracted by a jar of peanut butter, becomes separated from her family one night and must figure out how to find her way home. The story explores three fundamental spatial themes:

Retracing one's steps. In the story, Lucy discovers how to retrace her steps when she needs to find her way home. Kids might use this strategy to help them find their way around their school, or to find a toy or other object they lost somewhere in the house.

Interpreting a map. What makes a map such a powerful tool is that in it you see a larger area than what you can see from the ground. Looking at a map adds to your mental map of that environment. Of course, you first need to understand how to read a map, to interpret its unusual perspective and its scaled-down representation of features like streets, buildings, and landmarks. *Lucy in the City* introduces children to this new perspective through a literal bird's-eye view, when Lucy enlists an owl to help her figure out where to go.

Being aware of one's surroundings. Awareness of our surroundings helps us find our way around, lets us retrace our steps, and enables us to match up our mental map with the environment around us. Much like kids—who don't always have a say in where they go—at first, Lucy merely follows her family members in front of her, not paying attention to where she's going because she doesn't need to. But when Lucy is suddenly on her own, she starts to notice the smells, sights, and sounds around her, and gains an exciting new awareness of her surroundings.

How to Encourage Your Child's Spatial Thinking

Reading *Lucy in the City* with your child is a fun springboard from which you can explore a variety of types of spatial thinking. Start with the book: as you are reading and re-reading, take time to look at the illustrations and talk to your child about what happens in the story. Then use the prompts below to further exercise your spatial thinking muscles. For each type of spatial thinking, there are reading comprehension questions related to Lucy's story, a fun activity or game you can play with your child, and an "everyday practice" idea to help you integrate spatial thinking with things you and your child do throughout the day. In addition, following this Note, you will find additional activities, one related to each type of spatial thinking. These activities are also available for download at www.apa.org/pubs/magination/441B170.aspx.

The ideas below are described from the perspective of a parent or caregiver, but can also be adapted for the classroom. Note that some of the activities may be challenging for your child, or even for you. That's okay! Keep it fun, and go at your child's pace.

Spatial Relationships

Reading Comprehension

As you read the story with your child, or after you finish reading together, ask questions such as:
- "Which family member does Lucy follow when she goes out with her family?"
- "Why do you think that is?"
- "Where does Lucy's family live, and where do they go for food?"

Activity

Build a mini-city with blocks, magnetic tiles, or household items using the map in this book as inspiration. Use spatial language as you play with your child. For example: "Would this piece fit on top of that one?" "Let's make a wall around the whole thing." "Your house has a front door and a back door."

Everyday Practice

Notice and talk with your child about how things relate to one another in space. For example, at the dinner table (or in the classroom), who sits next to whom? Switch seats and talk about what's different about sitting somewhere else: Does your child have a different view now? A different neighbor? Or, while getting ready for school, talk about how your child arranges the stuff in his or her backpack or lunchbox so that everything fits.

Spatial Memory

Reading Comprehension

After you finish reading the story, ask your child:
- "What were the three places Lucy remembered that helped her retrace her steps and get home?"

Activity

Take a route you travel frequently, such as to and from school, and pick out landmarks along the way. Landmarks stand out; they are things you would use if you were giving someone directions—a unique building, a notable sign, a church on a corner, a park, or a school, for example. Develop a small set of landmarks with your child that you both can look out for along the way. Over time, as you travel the route, you can quiz each other on which landmark is coming up next, or where you make a turn.

Everyday Practice

The next time your child asks, "where is my...?" when looking for his stuff, take the opportunity to help your child practice re-tracing his steps. You can start with questions like, "when was the last time you were using it? Which room were you in?" For something very recently lost, have your child retrace his steps as closely as he can remember, looking out for the object on the ground or on surfaces where he might have set it down.

Spatial Representations

Reading Comprehension

Try asking your child questions such as:
- "How does the owl help Lucy find her way home?"
- "Why can the owl see places that she can't?"

Activity

Look at the maps in the story and ask your child if Lucy could have gotten to those destinations by taking other streets. See how many different routes you can find, and talk about how they are different—for example, some would take longer, or some would have more turns. Look at the complete map at the end of the story and find the movie theater, pond in the park, bakery, bridge, and Lucy's den. Is there anything else interesting that you notice about the map?

Everyday Practice

Work some simple maps and diagrams into your day. Draw or print out a map of a short trip, such as to school or the store, and have your child follow along during travel. Encourage your child to sketch out maps and diagrams. For example, you could ask your child for a drawing of who sat where at lunch, or a map sketch of his room.

Spatial Language

Reading Comprehension

Ask your child questions about the language in the book, such as:
- "Lucy and her family 'ran up streets, slinked down alleys, and tiptoed through backyards.' These are three different ways to describe what action?"
- "How are these descriptions similar, and how are they different?"

Activity

Try a hidden treasure game. Hide an object in the room, then give your child step-by-step directions that will lead him or her to it. For example, "Walk forward. Stop. Now turn to your right, towards the bookcase. Reach down. Open the cabinet door." Then switch roles: have your child hide the object and give you directions to find it.

Everyday Practice

Start noticing the spatial language you use in everyday speech, and make a point of using more. If you like, do an Internet search for "spatial language" for word lists.

Sense of Direction

Reading Comprehension

To help boost your child's sense of direction, try asking:

- "What does the owl say to Lucy to tell her where to go?"
- "Could the owl have described the directions in a different way?"
- "How do you know which way north, south, east, and west are on the map?"

Activity

Be a "human compass" and use your body to find the cardinal directions. On a sunny day, go outside in the middle of the day and stand so that you can see your shadow. Your back will be to the sun. Your shadow points north (as long as you are in the northern hemisphere). Extend your arms to each side, and hold out three fingers. Look for the one that makes an "E" in the shadow. That arm points east! Your other arm points west, and south is behind you. Note that in the morning hours, your shadow will point northwest, and in the late afternoon your shadow will point northeast. To find the exact cardinal directions, use a compass (your cell phone may have one).

Everyday Practice

Talk with your child about being lost. Common situations might include getting briefly separated from you in a store, or feeling disoriented when navigating the school campus. More unusual and intense situations would be getting lost in a busy theme park or on a hike in the wilderness. Discuss when Lucy's retrace-your-steps strategy would be good to try (at school, and perhaps in the store, if your child wanders away while you remain in the aisle or same part of the store), and when a strategy of staying put until someone comes to find you is safer (in a theme park, in the wilderness, and in the store if you're the one who has wandered away from your child). What other strategies could help in these situations? For example, you could shout or blow a whistle in the wilderness, or ask an appropriate adult for help in a store, theme park, or at school.

As adults, we use spatial thinking every day, usually without paying much attention unless we come up against a challenge—for example, finding an office we've never been to before, fitting all the groceries in one bag without breaking the eggs, or remembering where we left our keys. For kids, the questions, games, and activities presented above provide opportunities to practice different types of spatial thinking and improve these skills. Thinking spatially during play will help set kids up for success as they continue on through school and into their adult lives. And chances are, doing these activities with your child will enhance your own spatial skills, too!

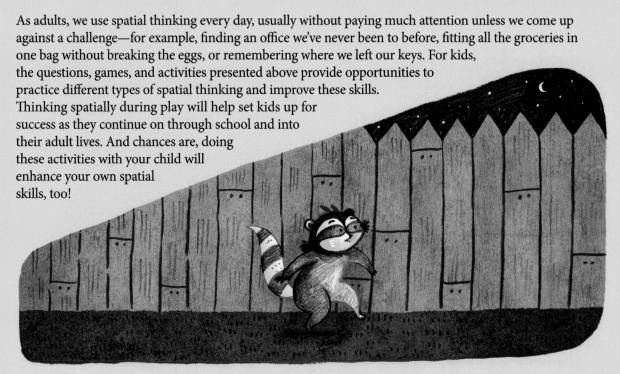

More Spatial Thinking Activities

Spatial Relationships

Can you find all seven objects hidden in this picture?

Spatial Memory

Lucy remembered three places on her way home: the movie theater, the pond in the park, and the bakery. Draw each one below, to help her get home!

Spatial Representations

Imagine you are the owl from the story. You are flying above your neighborhood, or your favorite playground, or the city where you live. Draw what things look like from high up above (your "bird's-eye view").

Spatial Language

Where is Lucy? Draw her surroundings to complete the scene.
Use your imagination, or draw a scene from the story.
1) Draw something in front of Lucy. 2) Draw something in
the air above Lucy's head. 3) Draw something under her feet.
4) Draw something behind Lucy.

Sense of Direction

Lucy is lost! Help her find her way to her den.

About the Author

Julie Dillemuth, PhD, is a spatial cognition geographer and children's writer. She is passionate about writing picture books for children that help develop spatial thinking skills. Her stories have appeared in *Highlights for Children* and *Odyssey* magazines.

About the Illustrator

Laura Wood's work can be found in picture books and magazines. By day, she likes to go in her studio to draw animals and little people. By night, she likes to put her dancing shoes on and lindy hop under the stars. There are three different places on this planet she calls home: Bristol, UK; Melbourne, Australia; and Treviglio, Italy.

About Magination Press

Magination Press is an imprint of the American Psychological Association, the largest scientific and professional organization representing psychologists in the United States and the largest association of psychologists worldwide.

For Clara, who notices everything.
Many thanks to Nora Newcombe, for helping Lucy find her home. *—JD*

For Giulia. I wish that you will happily wander the world and always find
your way back home. *—LW*

Published by
MAGINATION PRESS®
An Educational Publishing Foundation Book
American Psychological Association
750 First Street NE
Washington, DC 20002

Magination Press is a registered trademark of the American Psychological Association.

For more information about our books, including a complete catalog, please write to us, call 1-800-374-2721,
or visit our website at www.apa.org/pubs/magination.

Printed by Phoenix Color Corporation, Hagerstown, MD
Book design by Gwen Grafft

Library of Congress Cataloging-in-Publication Data

Dillemuth, Julie.
  Lucy in the city : a story about devleloping spatial thinking skills / by Julie Dillemuth, PhD ; illustrated by Laura Wood.
    pages cm
  "American Psychological Association."
  Summary: "A distracted young raccoon gets separated from her family one night. She discovers she can retrace her steps using
smells, sights, and sounds, plus help from an owl's birds'-eye view (which looks like a map). Focuses on developing spatial think-
ing, understanding the world around us, and using concepts of space for problem solving"— Provided by publisher.
    ISBN 978-1-4338-1927-8 (hardcover) — ISBN 1-4338-1927-9 (hardcover) — ISBN 978-1-4338-1928-5 (pbk.) — ISBN 1-4338-
1928-7 (pbk.) [1. Space perception—Fiction. 2. Lost children—Fiction. 3. Raccoon—Fiction.] I. Wood, Laura, 1985– illustrator.
II. Title.
  PZ7.1.D56Lu 2015
  [E]—dc23
                                            2014030252

Manufactured in the United States of America
First printing March 2015
10 9 8 7 6 5 4 3 2 1